RIP VAN WINKLE

Original story by Washington Irving

Retold by Jon Blake

Series Advisor Professor Kimberley Reynolds

Illustrated by Pep Boatella

OXFORD
UNIVERSITY PRESS

Letter from the Author

I was brought up in Southampton, where the big ships lived. My dad was an electrician and my mum worked in a shop. But I wanted to be a writer from the age of six. Either that or be prime minister. Sure enough, by the age of twenty, I was working in a shop.

Ten years later I did get a book published. Then another. Then another. Then ... you get the point. I now live in Cardiff with my partner Natalie and two amazing children. In my spare time I am a rock star, though not many people have noticed.

I was keen to rewrite *Rip Van Winkle* as it is a very famous story with a great idea behind it. I liked writing about Rip as he is absolutely nothing like me.

Jon Blake

Introduction

This story is set in exciting times. In 1775, settlers in America got fed up with being ruled by Britain and decided to rebel. They went to war and drove out the British after eight years of fighting. The United States of America was born.

Imagine living at that time and not even knowing a war was going on.

Welcome to the story of Rip Van Winkle.

Chapter One

Rip Van Winkle lives in a village at the foot of the Catskill Mountains. He's an easy-going man, who loves to go fishing with his dog, or entertain the village children. He's a good neighbour too. If you need a fence mending, Rip's your man.

Rip's own fences, however, are a mess. His farm is covered in weeds, and cows trample his cabbages.

The fact is, Rip doesn't like going home.

This isn't because of Rip's two children, Judith and Little Rip. Nor is it because of Wolf, his loyal dog. It's because of the monster in his house ...

... the monster called Dame Van Winkle.

Dame Van Winkle is Rip's wife. She is not a happy woman. She moans about her husband from noon till night. When she loses her temper, even Wolf runs for cover.

Rip has given up trying to fight back. He prefers to escape to the King George.

Chapter Two

The King George is the village inn. It's named after the King of Great Britain. On the day our story starts, Rip is sitting outside it with the men of the village.

'These new taxes are wrong!' declares Jans, the innkeeper. 'All taxes should be agreed by the people!'

'We must show the King he can't push us around!' says Boon, the historian.

'What are we? Mice or men?' says Dirks, the schoolmaster.

‘Help!’ squeaks Rip. ‘My wife!’

Dame Van Winkle storms up. ‘Rip!’ she cries. ‘I knew I’d find you here! Now get to your useless farm and cut me a cabbage!’

Rip dutifully follows his wife back to his farm. Wolf joins him, whining. Seeing his poor dog looking so glum, Rip feels terribly sorry. He fetches his shotgun.

‘Come on, boy,’ he says. ‘Let’s go for a walk.’

It is late afternoon, and the Catskills are covered in a blue haze. They seem full of promise and magic. Rip and Wolf climb higher and higher until they reach a grassy peak. They look down over the majestic River Hudson. This was named after Hendrick Hudson, the great explorer who discovered it. Rip falls into a daydream: he imagines Hudson's ship sailing up the river, over a hundred years ago.

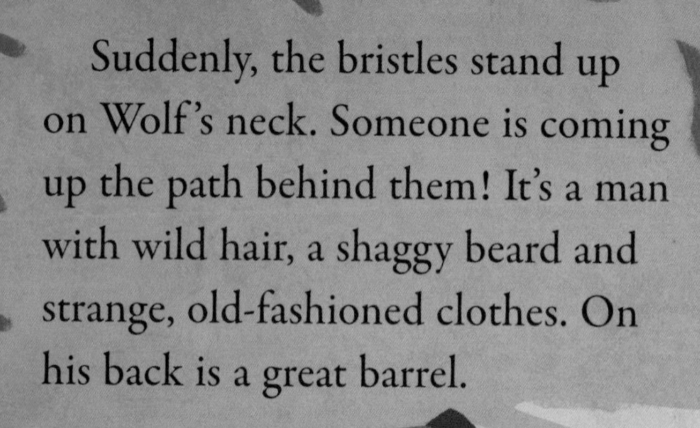

Suddenly, the bristles stand up on Wolf's neck. Someone is coming up the path behind them! It's a man with wild hair, a shaggy beard and strange, old-fashioned clothes. On his back is a great barrel.

Wolf begins to growl. Rip thinks about running away. But the man is struggling, and Rip just *has* to help him.

'Let's take turns carrying this barrel,' Rip suggests.

Rip takes the barrel from the wild-bearded man, who does not utter a word of thanks.

Chapter Three

The two men set off up a narrow rocky path. Wolf follows nervously. It's a hard climb. The two men take turns carrying the barrel, in complete silence.

Finally the bearded man stops. They have come to a flat patch of land, surrounded by huge cliffs. Wolf runs forward, then stops dead. More bearded men!

There must be twenty of them. They wear old-fashioned baggy trousers, like the barrel man. They also have peculiar faces, slightly green, with tired sunken eyes. One man seems to be in charge. Perhaps that is because he is the weirdest of all, with a deeply wrinkled face, high hat and red stockings.

At first, the men do not notice Rip and Wolf. Their minds are fixed on a game of skittles. It is a deadly serious business. There is no sound except the clack of ball on skittle, echoing around the mountain:

Suddenly the action stops. Someone has noticed Rip. The men turn. Their staring eyes are as dead as stone.

'Good evening,' says Rip.

Not one reply.

'I come in peace,' says Rip.

The leader points a finger. Is he pointing at me, wonders Rip? But no, he is pointing at the barrel. The wild-bearded man pulls a cork from it. An aroma of pine and walnuts fills the air. The barrel contains a strange liquid which the man begins to empty into stone jars.

Rip seizes the chance to be useful. He takes a jar and nervously approaches the leader.

'Would you like some, er ... ?' he begins.

The leader snatches the jar and downs the contents in one.

'Anyone else?' asks Rip.

No reply. Rip serves them anyway. Like the leader, they drink thirstily. When every drop is drained, they go back to their skittles.

Rip begins to relax. He starts to wonder about the strange potion. What does it taste like? Surely one sip would do no harm.

One jar remains. Rip picks it up. No one is bothered. Slowly Rip brings it to his mouth and takes just a little taste.

The potion is heavenly!

Hmm, thinks Rip. *Just one more sip ...*

Rip takes another sip. Then another. Then another. Rip tips back the stone jar and downs the lot.

Suddenly Rip begins to feel tired.

'Wolf,' he begins. 'We really must ... '

Rip never finishes the sentence. He has fallen into a deep, deep sleep.

Chapter Four

The sun is shining when Rip's eyes reopen. 'I've slept all night!' he gasps. There is no sign of the skittle gang. Rip's gun is also missing. In its place is a useless rusting weapon which has obviously been left as a joke.

'Wolf!' cries Rip.

No answer.

Dame Van Winkle will kill me! thinks Rip. He tries to jump up, but his body is as stiff as a board. It takes him a full minute to get to his feet.

Everything looks different. The rocky path has gone, replaced by a gushing stream. The grassy peak is covered in bushes. And no matter how loud Rip whistles, there is no sign of Wolf.

Maybe he's gone home, thinks Rip. But when he reaches the village, that has changed as well.

There are more houses, and children that he has never seen before. None of them welcome him. They simply stroke their chins and laugh.

Rip feels his own chin.

Jumping jellybeans!

His beard is a foot long!

What was in that potion?

With growing panic, Rip makes his way back home. Whatever will the Dame say?

But there is no sign of her. The house is empty and the roof has fallen in. A half-starved dog prowls nearby.

'Wolf?' murmurs Rip.

The dog snarls.

'Someone tell me what's going on!' cries Rip. His voice echoes round the lonely remains of his house.

Rip hurries to the King George. The inn has been replaced by a hotel. The sign says 'George Washington' instead of 'King George'. Hanging nearby is a strange flag of stars and stripes.

A crowd begins to gather around Rip. A posh man with a silver cane pushes through. 'What's the idea of coming here with a gun?' he demands.

'Fear not,' replies Rip. 'I'm a loyal subject of the King.'

The crowd gasps. 'A royalist!' cries one man.

'A spy!' cries another.

'Don't you know King George doesn't rule here any more,' says a third.

'What are you doing here?' asks the posh man.

'I live here!' protests Rip. 'Does no one know Rip Van Winkle?'

'Rip Van Winkle?' repeats a woman. 'That's Rip Van Winkle!' She points at a ragged young man leaning against a tree. He seems strangely familiar to Rip, though he can't say why.

'So who are you?' says the man.

'I knew yesterday,' says Rip, 'but now I'm not so sure.'

Chapter Five

'Arrest him!' cries a voice in the crowd. Just then, another woman pushes through, carrying a baby.

'Wait!' she says. 'I think I've seen this man before.'

Rip studies the woman. 'And I think I've seen you before,' he replies, 'though I can't think where.'

'He's playing for time!' cries another voice.

'Arrest him!' says a second. Others take up the cry, which becomes so loud that the baby cries too.

‘Control yourselves!’ says the woman. ‘You’re upsetting Little Rip!’

Rip Van Winkle is astonished. ‘Another Rip?’ he says. ‘How many Rips are there in this village?’

‘We named him after my father,’ replied the woman. ‘Twenty years ago he left for the mountains. We never saw him again.’

Rip stares into the woman’s face.

No … it couldn’t be

… could it?

‘Are you ... Judith?’ he asks.

The baying crowd fall silent.

‘How did you know?’ asks the woman.

‘You ... are my daughter!’ cries Rip.

‘Dad?’ says the woman.

‘Dad?’ says the young man lounging against the tree.

All three hug. ‘But I don’t understand!’ says Rip. ‘I only went to the mountains yesterday!’

‘Believe me, Dad,’ says Judith. ‘It really has been twenty years.’

At this point a frail old man makes himself known. 'Rip,' he says. 'It's Peter Boon, the historian.'

'Peter?' replies Rip. 'But you look so old!'

'Tell me, Rip,' says Boon. 'Did you meet anyone in the mountains?'

Rip tells the whole story. The strange bearded men ... the skittles ... the potion ...

'Great heavens!' says Boon. 'Then the stories are true.'

‘What stories?’ asks Rip.

‘They say,’ says Boon, ‘that every twenty years, Hendrick Hudson comes back with his men. Even in death, they cannot abandon the land they discovered.’

A chill goes down Rip’s spine. Has he really met the famous Hudson? Then it is not so hard to believe he has slept for twenty years!

'Judith!' he cries. 'Little Rip! Even Littler Rip! We have so much time to make up for! I shall rebuild the house and ... ' A sudden thought strikes him. 'But where is Dame Van Winkle?' he asks.

'Sadly,' says Judith, 'she is no more.'

Rip nods gravely, but inside he is rejoicing.

This really is a new America! thinks Rip. From now on, his house will be happy, his farm will be fertile, and nothing will disturb his peace – except, maybe, that unearthly sound from the Catskill Mountains:

CLACK!

CLACK!

CLACK!